©2001 Great Smoky Mountains Association

Story, illustration, and design by Lisa Horstman

Edited by Karen Ballentine, Kent Cave, and Steve Kemp

Project Coordination by Steve Kemp

The author wishes to thank the following for their help during the research of this book: Jay Clark, Scott Gatewood, Jennifer Hartsog, Patrick McEachern, Jennifer Pierce, William Puckett, William Stiver, Brandon Wear, Karen Wade, Jim Sexton, and Coury Turczyn.

Printed in China
   12 13 14 15 16 17 18 19 20
Published by Great Smoky Mountains Association, a nonprofit organization assisting Great Smoky Mountains National Park since 1953.
P.O. Box 130, Gatlinburg, TN 37738.
(888) 898-9102
www.SmokiesInformation.org
All purchases benefit the park.

About the author
Lisa Horstman lives and works in Knoxville, Tennessee, in sight of the Great Smoky Mountains. This is her third children's book. Her first, *Fast Friends*, won the prestigious Dr. Seuss Picture Book Award. Her second, *The Great Smoky Mountain Salamander Ball*, received the award for interpretive excellence from the National Park Service. She is a member of The Authors Guild, Inc., and The Authors League of America, Inc.

This book is for my brother, Dan, and my sisters, Kay, Pat, and Sue; their humor and life lessons are a big part of who I am today. *Atta boy, Luther!* It's also for Dave, as always. —*LH*

the Troublesome Cub

words & pictures by Lisa Horstman

A hungry black bear parts branches in her way
Just after sunrise one fine sunny day.
Not too far behind, a little bear cub
Makes mischief and mayhem and general hubbub.

Both bears are hungry
as breakfast time beckons,
Cub chews one berry...
and then eats a second.

Soon they find acorns
upon which to feast
And roots and some insects—
good food for a beast!

The sun rises high in the late-summer sky
Both bellies are full; now it's time for shut-eye.

Or so Mother thought, but around her, Cub prances.
A swat of Mom's paw puts a halt to his dances.

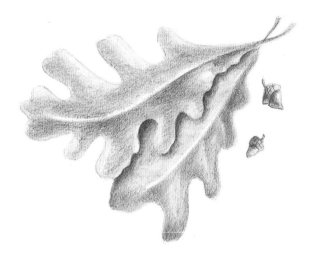

They settle below a small grove of green trees,
Soon all that's stirring are leaves in the breeze.
Late afternoon shadows take over the sun
The golden air touches each bear, one by one.

First a stir, then a wiggle, now Bear Cub's awake!
Wake up! Wake up! He gives Mother a shake.
With a sleepy black paw she warns him away
So Cub ambles off to frolic and play.

He scrambles along through the flowers and shrubs
A lot to explore for one small bear cub.
Bees zip around him. There's honey nearby!
They soon fly away to the darkening sky.

But Cub forges on—this is way too much fun!
He'll travel for miles before he's quite done.
Poking his snout to the late summer breeze
An odor floats by him that seems sure to please.

The promise of food beckons Cub to a street
That Cub has to cross, for it leads to a treat.
With the park now behind him and town straight ahead,
Cub thinks with his stomach instead of his head.

The scent pulls him nearer, then closer than close
Until he feels dizzy with smell overdose!
A green metal trash bin contains his great prize
Mountains of garbage all coated with flies.

Cub takes a nosedive right into the pile
And makes greedy bear plans to stay there awhile.
Cellophane wrapping with food sticking to it,
A fast food container—Cub ate right through it!

So what if it's plastic? A bear doesn't know
that he shouldn't eat fast food containers, although
It smells like good eating, looks like a fine meal,
And fills up his belly. It sure seems ideal.

So he gorges on garbage and falls fast asleep
inside the container, way down in the heap.

A rumbling wakes him just after sunrise
And he's tossed in a truck,
much to his surprise.

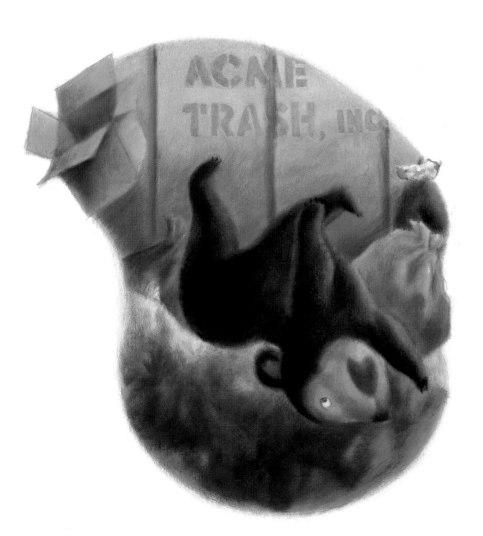

Now this is adventure
he doesn't much care for,
Every bump in the road makes
him grunt and despair more.
And the garbage he cherished
so much at the start
Makes him sick to his stomach
and heavy of heart.

His mother's awake now and wringing her paws,
She worries and wonders just what is the cause
Of her little son's wandering far from his home,
Away from park safety to places unknown.

Stuck in the darkness,
Cub feels the truck stop.
Then—sliding and tumbling
and flippity-flop!
The garbage folks hear him,
and to their surprise
The garbage before them
contains two bright eyes!

Cub whirls in a panic
while trailing decay,
and makes rotten food fly
every which way.
He runs through a doorway,
leaps onto a beam
Holds on for dear life,
then lets out a scream!

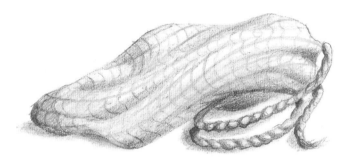

Trapped on a rafter, Cub sees with a frown,
He can't move a muscle and hangs upside-down!
Below him the workers all stand in a knot
Below *them*, the garbage continues to rot.

Nobody knows what the next step is now,
They know they must help him, but no one knows how.
A ranger arrives, and with him, a net.
Rescuing Bear Cub may still happen yet.

He twirls the net all around his big hat,
It circles around Bear Cub before he falls flat.
There's no time to waste as Bear Cub still dangles,
Cub's leg and the rafter must still be untangled.

Into the rafters the park ranger crawls
to save one small bear from a treacherous fall.
He slowly and gently untwists Bear Cub's paw
And it looks like Bear Cub will be saved, after all.

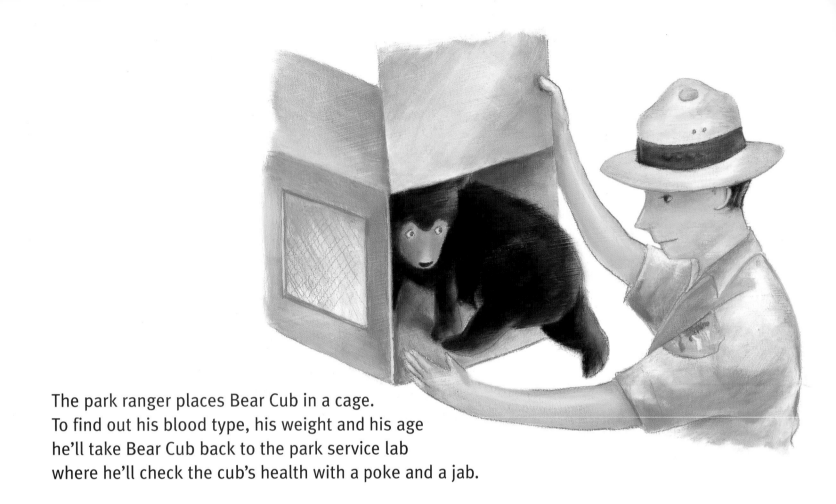

The park ranger places Bear Cub in a cage.
To find out his blood type, his weight and his age
he'll take Bear Cub back to the park service lab
where he'll check the cub's health with a poke and a jab.

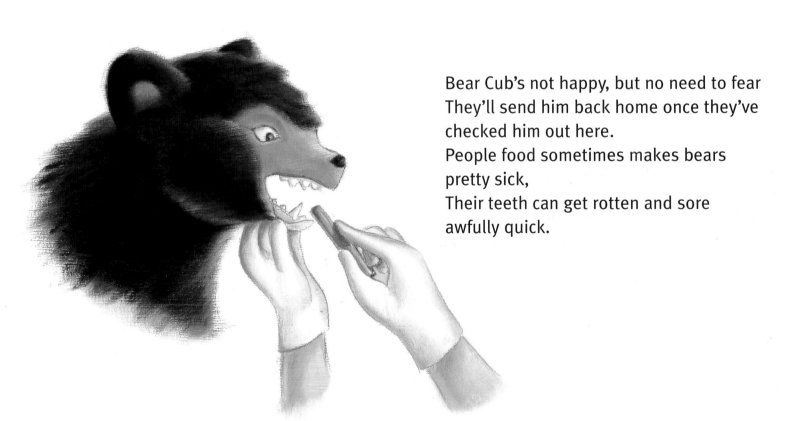

Bear Cub's not happy, but no need to fear
They'll send him back home once they've checked him out here.
People food sometimes makes bears pretty sick,
Their teeth can get rotten and sore awfully quick.

So that rangers can track him in mountain and holler,
They circle his neck with a radio collar
All for the purpose of tracking his tracks
To check where he goes when he's snacking his snacks.

Luckily, Bear Cub's okay through it all—
A little shook up from his scary close call.
He'd rather hang out with his mom in the woods.
With humans, he tends to be misunderstood.

Finally, it's time to return to the wild,
Time to unite the mother and child,
The cage door is opened. Here's freedom at last!
Cub leaps into sunshine and wilderness fast.

And so, Bear Cub learned a hard lesson that day
Of not eating leftover human buffet.
Yes, he learned his lesson—have we learned one too?
Or maybe it's something we already knew.

Because it's our job to take care of the earth
Since everything on it has some sort of worth.
A good way to start is to not let the bears
Get our leftover burgers and chocolate eclairs.

A hungry black bear parts branches in her way
Just before sunset one fine sunny day.
Bear Cub runs toward her, so glad to be home
And into the woods they continue to roam.

When I am in Bear Country, I promise to:

• Put all trash and food scraps in bear-proof trash bins, and close the lid tight!

• Store coolers and picnic baskets in the car at night and when not in use.

• Pick up litter and food scraps.

• Never feed wild animals.